You Can't Take a Balloon

y

1-10-02			
OCT 2 2 2004			
FEB 0 8 2005			
MAR 1 8 2005			

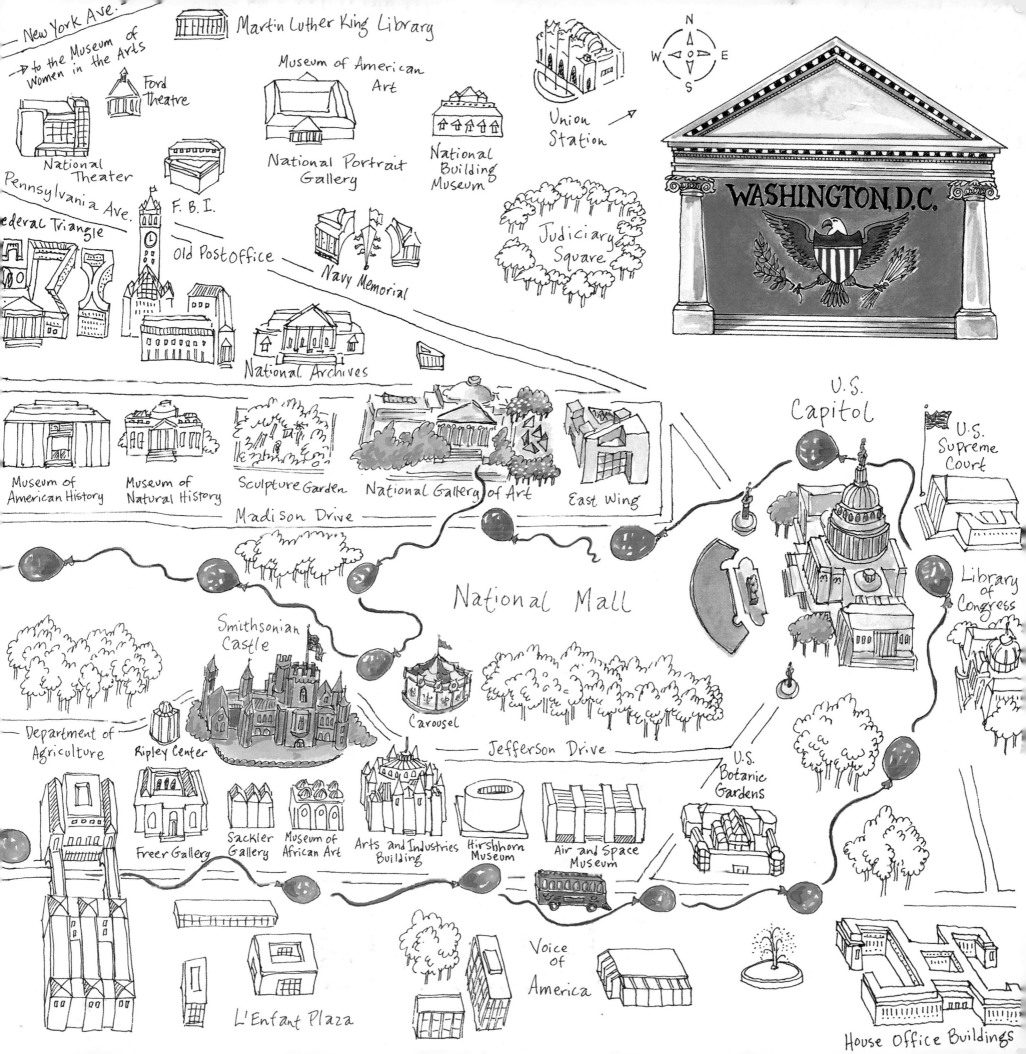

You Can't Take a Balloon Into The National Gallery

story by Jacqueline Preiss Weitzman
pictures by Robin Preiss Glasser

PUFFIN BOOKS

To our father, Ralph Preiss, whose unabashed love for the United States,

his adopted country, greatly influenced the way we think and feel.

–J.P.W. and R.P.G.

PUFFIN BOOKS

Published by the Penguin Group

Penguin Putnam Books for Young Readers,

345 Hudson Street, New York, New York 10014, U.S.A.

Penguin Books Ltd, 80 Strand, London WC2R 0RL, England

Penguin Books Australia Ltd, Ringwood, Victoria, Australia

Penguin Books Canada Ltd, 10 Alcorn Avenue, Toronto, Ontario, Canada M4V 3B2

Penguin Books (N.Z.) Ltd, 182-190 Wairau Road, Auckland 10, New Zealand

Penguin Books Ltd, Registered Offices: Harmondsworth, Middlesex, England

First published in the United States of America by Dial Books for Young Readers,

a division of Penguin Putnam Books for Young Readers, 2000

Published by Puffin Books, a division of Penguin Putnam Books for Young Readers, 2002

1 3 5 7 9 10 8 6 4 2

Copyright © Jacqueline Preiss Weitzman and Robin Preiss Glasser, 2000

THE LIBRARY OF CONGRESS HAS CATALOGED THE DIAL EDITION AS FOLLOWS:

Weitzman, Jacqueline Preiss

You can't take a balloon into the National Gallery / story by Jacqueline Preiss Weitzman; pictures by Robin Preiss Glasser.

p. cm.

Summary: While a brother and sister, along with their grandmother, visit the National Gallery of Art, the balloon they were
not allowed to bring into the museum floats around Washington, D.C., causing a series of mishaps at various tourist sites.

ISBN 0-8037-2303-2

1. Washington (D.C.)–Juvenile fiction. 2. National Gallery of Art (U.S.)–Juvenile fiction. [1. Washington (D.C.)–Fiction.
2. National Gallery of Art (U.S.)–Fiction. 3. Balloons–Fiction. 4. Stories without words] I. Glasser, Robin Preiss, ill. II. Title.

PZ7.W4481843Yr 2000 [E]–dc21 99-36367 CIP

The artwork was prepared using black ink, watercolor washes, gouache, and colored pencils.

Puffin Books ISBN 0-14-230131-0

Printed in Hong Kong

TAKE YOUR
PHOTO
WITH
GEORGE

our camera: $6.–
your camera: $4.–

GALLERY O

8

ELEVATOR
OUT OF ORDER
Please
use stairs →
CAUTION:
THERE ARE 898
STAIRS TO THE TOP

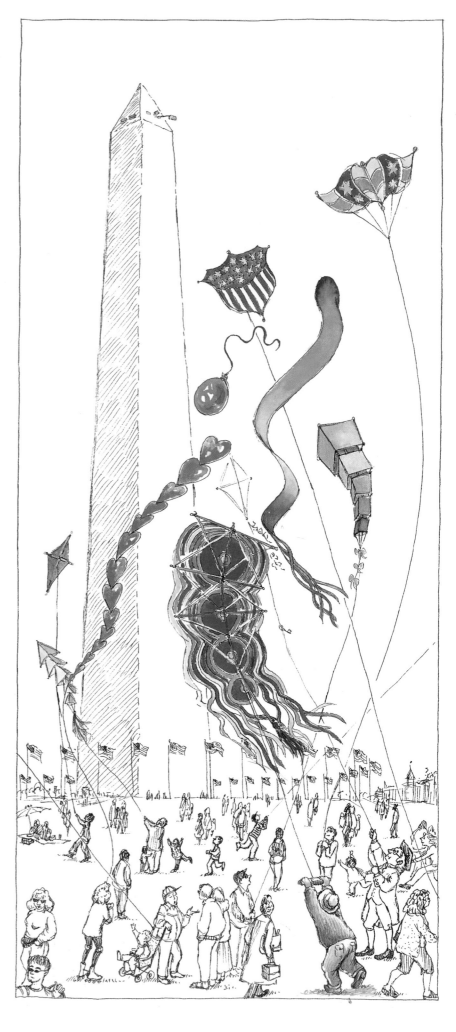

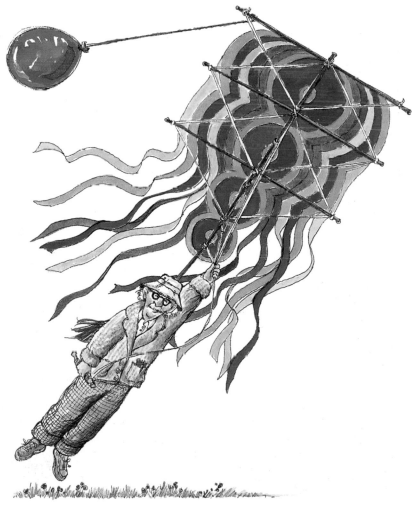

Prohibited Inside the White House

No firecrackers or fireworks	No guns or ammunition	No animals (except guide dogs)
No balloons	No videotaping	No knives with blades over 3"/8cm
No nunchucks	No smoking	No mace

ÉDOUARD MANET

VISITORS ENTRANCE
Quiet Please
NO SMOKING

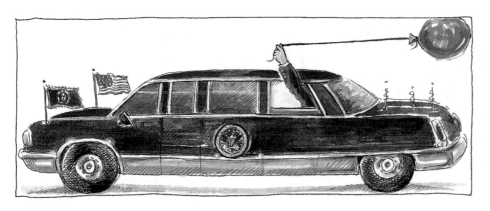

Acknowledgments

The author and artist would like to thank the following people for all of their help and support in making this book possible:

At the National Gallery of Art: Ira Bartfield, Chief of Visual Services; Nancy Stanfield and Barbara Goldstein, Photographic Rights and Reproductions; Sara Sanders-Buell, Picture Researcher; Carlotta Owens, Department of Modern Prints and Drawings.

In Washington, D.C.: Susan Huntting, Director of Constituent Services for Senator Barbara Boxer; Jacquie Simpson, Washington Jaycees; Albert Gaswell, U.S. Capitol; Dr. Betty Ann Ottinger; Ann Stock; Elise Lipoff; Carolyn Chabrow Berger.

At Dial Books for Young Readers: Toby Sherry, Editor; Atha Tehon, Art Director; Kimi Weart, Designer; Julie Rauer, Designer; Regina Castillo, Senior Production Editor; Phyllis J. Fogelman.

We would also like to express our appreciation to our agent, Faith Hornby Hamlin; Janet Hicks, Artists Rights Society, Ann Prival, VAGA; as well as Larry Weitzman, Erica Regunberg, Suzanne Molera, and Judy Weitzman.

List of works of art reproduced from the collections of the National Gallery of Art

Francesco Righetti, Attributed to, After Giovanni Bologna, "Mercury," c. 1780/1800 (page 11), Andrew W. Mellon Collection, Photograph © 1998 Board of Trustees, National Gallery of Art, Washington.

Jasper Francis Cropsey, "The Spirit of War," 1851 (page 12), Avalon Fund, Photograph © 1998 Board of Trustees, National Gallery of Art, Washington.

Constantin Brancusi, "Bird in Space," 1925 (page 14), Gift of Eugene and Agnes E. Meyer, Photograph © 1998 Board of Trustees, National Gallery of Art, Washington. © 1999 Artists Rights Society (ARS), New York/ADAGP, Paris.

Alexander Calder, "Untitled," 1976 (page 17), Gift of the Collectors Committee, Photograph © 1998 Board of Trustees, National Gallery of Art, Washington. © 1999 Estate of Alexander Calder/Artists Rights Society (ARS), New York.

Édouard Manet, "The Railway," 1873 (page 19), Gift of Horace Havemeyer in memory of his mother, Louisine W. Havemeyer, Photograph © 1998 Board of Trustees, National Gallery of Art, Washington.

Wayne Thiebaud, "Cakes," 1963 (page 21), Gift in Honor of the 50th Anniversary of the National Gallery of Art from the Collectors Committee, the 50th Anniversary Gift Committee, and The Circle, with Additional Support from the Abrams Family in Memory of Harry N. Abrams, Photograph © 1998 Board of Trustees, National Gallery of Art, Washington.

Winslow Homer, "Right and Left," 1909 (page 23), Gift of the Avalon Foundation, Photograph © 1998 Board of Trustees, National Gallery of Art, Washington.

Henri Matisse, "Large Composition with Masks," 1953 (page 24), Ailsa Mellon Bruce Fund, Photograph © 1998 Board of Trustees, National Gallery of Art, Washington. © 1999 Succession H. Matisse, Paris/Artists Rights Society (ARS), New York.

Edgar Degas, "Four Dancers," c. 1899 (page 26), Chester Dale Collection, Photograph © 1998 Board of Trustees, National Gallery of Art, Washington.

Auguste Rodin, "The Thinker," 1880 (page 28), Gift of Mrs. John W. Simpson, Photograph © 1998 Board of Trustees, National Gallery of Art, Washington.

André Derain, "Charing Cross Bridge, London," 1906 (page 29), John Hay Whitney Collection, Photograph © 1998 Board of Trustees, National Gallery of Art, Washington. © 1999 Artists Rights Society (ARS), New York/ADAGP, Paris.

George Bellows, "Both Members of This Club," 1909 (page 31), Chester Dale Collection, Photograph © 1998 Board of Trustees, National Gallery of Art, Washington.

Jasper Johns, "Flags I," 1973 (page 34), Robert and Jane Meyerhoff Collection, Photograph © 1998 Board of Trustees, National Gallery of Art, Washington. © Jasper Johns/Licensed by VAGA, New York, NY.

Faces from History

While spending time in Washington, D.C., to research this book, we couldn't help but feel the presence of many of the great men and women who made their mark on that city and the history and lore of this country. We enjoyed placing some of their images in scenes throughout the book. We hope you have just as much fun spotting them. (This list is not meant to be comprehensive, and represents only our personal choices.)

—J.P.W. and R.P.G.

page 13: bottom right panel—running with rolls of plans under his arm
Pierre Charles L'Enfant (1754–1825) A veteran of the American Revolution, this French-born engineer and architect designed the basic plan for Washington, D.C. After being dismissed from the project for political reasons by President George Washington in 1792, he took his plans with him, but his grand vision for a new capital city was realized by those who succeeded him.

page 13: bottom right—wearing a Rough Riders uniform
Theodore Roosevelt (1858–1919) A writer, explorer, and soldier, in 1898 he organized the first regiment U.S. volunteer cavalry known as the Rough Riders to fight in the Spanish-American War. He became the twenty-sixth President of the United States in 1901 and served two terms (1901–1909).

page 14: left panel—behind picnickers, with surveying equipment
Benjamin Banneker (1731–1806) This astronomer, mathematician, inventor, writer, and compiler of almanacs worked with Andrew Ellicott on the planning of Washington, D.C. After L'Enfant's dismissal, he reconstructed the lost plans for the new capital city from memory.

page 16: right panel—wearing a three-corner hat and flying a traditional diamond-shaped kite
Benjamin Franklin (1706–1790) One of America's Founding Fathers, this printer, publisher, author, inventor, and diplomat was also an accomplished scientist. His experiments in electricity included flying a kite in a thunderstorm, which led to the development of the lightning rod.

page 18: walking on sidewalk with a watering can
Lady Bird Johnson (b. 1912) As the wife of President Lyndon B. Johnson, her work included promoting highway and civic beautification projects around the country.

page 18: sitting behind woman with dog, looking through the fence at the White House
Richard M. Nixon (1913–1994) He was the thirty-seventh President of the United States (1969–1974), and is known for, among other things, opening relations with Communist China and being the first U.S. President to resign from office.

page 19: bottom panel—standing at Visitors Entrance to the White House
Jacqueline Bouvier Kennedy (1929–1994) The wife of President John F. Kennedy, she was responsible for the restoration of the White House and filling it with authentic American furnishings and art.

page 20: top right panel—in lace bonnet, standing behind camera man
Dolley Madison (1768–1849) President James Madison's wife, she is best remembered for saving many important state papers, as well as the Gilbert Stuart painting of George Washington (seen on page 20) when the White House was burned down during the British invasion of Washington, D.C., in the War of 1812.

page 20: bottom right panel—standing to the left of the American flag
John Adams (1735–1826) This Founding Father served as the first Vice President of the United States (1789–1797) under George Washington, and as the second President of the United States (1797–1801). He was the first President to live in the White House.

page 21: top panel—enjoying the party behind man in chef's hat
John F. Kennedy (1917–1963) The thirty-fifth President of the United States (1961–1963), he was considered the first to benefit from television as a major factor in an election.

page 21: bottom left panel—conductor with baton
John Philip Sousa (1854–1932) Known as the March King, this composer of military marches was the leader of the U.S. Marine Band from 1880 to 1892.

page 22: standing with wife, Nancy, behind dueling sound man
Ronald Reagan (b. 1911) As the fortieth President of the United States (1981–1989), he promoted a popular Conservative agenda, including the "Star Wars" defense program. He was also the first President to have been a professional actor.

page 22: standing to the right of her husband
Nancy Reagan (b. 1914) As the wife of President Ronald Reagan, she was a proponent of the "Just say no" antidrug program.

page 22: to the left of the Reagans, smoking a pipe
Andrew Jackson (1767–1845) Known as Old Hickory, this seventh President of the United States (1829–1837) was the first to be elected from the area west of the Appalachians, and the first to gain office by popular vote. After the inauguration of the "people's president," crowds of enthusiastic supporters attended the open house at the Executive Mansion and left it in ruins.

page 22: to the left of the flagpole, wearing a hat
Franklin Delano Roosevelt (1882–1945) Elected in 1933, this thirty-second President of the United States was the first and only to serve three terms and be elected to a fourth. From 1933 to 1945, he led the country through the Great Depression and the Second World War.

page 24: top panel—walking with his wife, Rosalynn, in the parade, behind the horses
Jimmy Carter (b. 1924) This thirty-ninth President of the United States (1977–1981) was active in negotiating the Camp David Accords (signed in 1979), which

ended a thirty-one-year state of war between Israel and Egypt. He was the first President to walk from the Capitol to the White House after his inauguration.

page 24: top panel—walking arm in arm with her husband
Rosalynn Carter (b. 1927) As President Jimmy Carter's First Lady, she was the first to visit foreign nations alone as an official representative of the administration.

page 26: top panel—standing at far right of parade, looking to see where she can help
Clara Barton (1821–1912) Known as the Angel of the Battlefield for her relief work during the Civil War and later in the Franco-Prussian and Spanish-American wars, she organized the American Red Cross in 1881.

page 27: top left panel—walking Fala the dog
Eleanor Roosevelt (1884–1962) The wife of President Franklin Delano Roosevelt, she broke new ground by becoming famous in her own right and engaging actively in public life. After her husband's death, she continued to devote herself to national and international humanitarian interests, and served as a delegate to the United Nations General Assembly from 1945–1953, and again in 1961. She was often referred to as the First Lady of the World.

page 27: top left panel—walking Socks the cat
Hillary Rodham Clinton (b. 1947) As the wife of Bill Clinton, the forty-second President of the United States (1993–2001), she modeled her role as First Lady after Eleanor Roosevelt. She participated actively in many areas of public life, most notably health care, child care, education, and women's rights.

page 27: bottom left panel—in crowd on right with dark whiskers
Abraham Lincoln (1809–1865) Honest Abe was the sixteenth President of the United States (1861–1865). He is famous not only for his integrity, eloquence, and strong leadership during the Civil War, but also for signing the Emancipation Proclamation, which eventually led to the Thirteenth Amendment and the abolition of slavery.

page 28: bottom panel—standing on stairs of Lincoln Memorial in long gown
Marian Anderson (1897–1993) This African-American singer and alternate delegate to the United Nations was considered to be one of the finest contraltos of her time. After being denied access to Washington's Constitution Hall because of her race, she was invited by Eleanor Roosevelt to sing on the steps of the Lincoln Memorial, which she did on Easter Sunday 1939 before a crowd of 75,000. This was considered a major victory for the early civil rights movement.

page 29: top left panel—walking on bridge behind trolley
Thomas Jefferson (1743–1826) This Founding Father was the principal author of the Declaration of Independence. He was the first Secretary of State (1790–1794), the second Vice President (1797–1801), and the third President of the United States (1801–1809).

page 29: bottom right panel—in judicial robes on the steps of the Capitol
Thurgood Marshall (1908–1993) In 1954 he successfully argued the case of *Brown v. Board of Education of Topeka* before the Supreme Court, in which racial segregation in public schools was declared unconstitutional. In 1967 President Lyndon B. Johnson appointed him the first African-American justice of the United States Supreme Court.

page 29: bottom right panel—in judicial robes on the steps of the Capitol
Sandra Day O'Connor (b. 1930) In 1981 President Ronald Reagan nominated her to the United States Supreme Court, and she became the first woman to serve as an associate justice.

page 29: bottom right panel—sitting on steps (in left corner) of the Capitol with Susan B. Anthony
Elizabeth Cady Stanton (1815–1902) A reformer who stood for equal education, suffrage, and property rights for women, she organized the first women's rights convention in 1848 in Seneca Falls, New York.

page 29: bottom right panel—standing on steps of the Capitol to the left of Elizabeth Cady Stanton
Susan B. Anthony (1820–1906) This teacher was a pioneer in the women's suffrage movement. Working closely with her friend Elizabeth Cady Stanton in demanding equal civil and voting rights for women, her work helped lead the way to the Nineteenth Amendment to the Constitution, passed in 1920, which gave women the right to vote.

page 30: top right panel—in profile to the left of the family with baby
James Madison (1751–1836) This Founding Father was the fourth President of the United States (1809–1817). During the War of 1812, he became the first and only President to actively exercise his authority as commander-in-chief, leading a battery to stall the capture of Washington by the British.

page 30: top right panel—to the right of the family with the baby
Madeleine Albright (b. 1937) In 1997 President Bill Clinton appointed her as the first woman Secretary of State of the United States.

page 30: bottom left panel—standing in bottom right-hand corner, shaking hands with President Lyndon B. Johnson
Martin Luther King, Jr. (1929–1968) Winner of the Nobel Peace Prize in 1964, this eloquent Baptist minister led the civil rights movement from the mid-1950's until his assassination in 1968. His work led President Lyndon B. Johnson to sign the Civil Rights Act of 1964, which attacked racial segregation in public places and schools, and racial discrimination in employment.

page 30: bottom left panel—shaking hands with Dr. Martin Luther King, Jr.
Lyndon B. Johnson (1908–1973) The thirty-sixth President of the United States (1963–1969), he initiated many important social service programs in education, housing, urban development, transportation, and environmental conservation. Besides signing the Civil Rights Act of 1964, he also signed the Medicare Bill of 1965, which created a system of health care for the elderly under the Social Security program.

page 34: top left panel—looking at reporter with cellular phone
Alexander Graham Bell (1847–1922) This Scottish-born audiologist was best known as the inventor of the telephone. He served as the president of the National Geographic Society and lived in Washington, D.C., for many years.